AUG 2 1 2017

SANTA ANA PUBLIC LIBRARY

D1177606

Mi visita al dentista

My Visit to the Dentist

David Lee

traducido por / translated by

Eida de la Vega

ilustrado por / illustrated by

Anita Morra

PowerKiDS
press.

New York

Published in 2017 by The Rosen Publishing Group, Inc.
29 East 21st Street, New York, NY 10010

Copyright © 2017 by The Rosen Publishing Group, Inc.

All rights reserved. No part of this book may be reproduced in any form without permission in writing from the publisher, except by a reviewer.

First Edition

Translator: Eida de la Vega
Editorial Director, Spanish: Nathalie Beullens-Maoui
Editor, English: Caitie McAneney
Book Design: Michael Flynn
Illustrator: Anita Morra

Cataloging-in-Publication Data

Names: Lee, David, 1990- author.
Title: My visit to the dentist = Mi visita al dentista / David Lee.
Description: New York : PowerKids Press, [2017] | Series: Community helpers = Trabajadores de la comunidad | In English and Spanish | Includes index.
Identifiers: ISBN 9781499430387 (library bound book)
Subjects: LCSH: Dentistry–Juvenile literature. | Teeth–Care and
  hygiene–Juvenile literature.
Classification: LCC RK63 .L44 2017 | DDC 617.6–dc23

Manufactured in the United States of America

CPSIA Compliance Information: Batch #BW17PK: For Further Information contact Rosen Publishing, New York, New York at 1-800-237-9932

Contenido

Contents

Tengo que hacerme una limpieza dental.
Voy al dentista.

It's time to get my teeth cleaned.

I go to the dentist.

Me siento en una silla grande.

I sit in a big chair

La dentista se sienta a mi lado.

The dentist sits next to me.

La dentista enciende una luz
brillante. Mira dentro de mi boca.
¡Di *ahhh*!

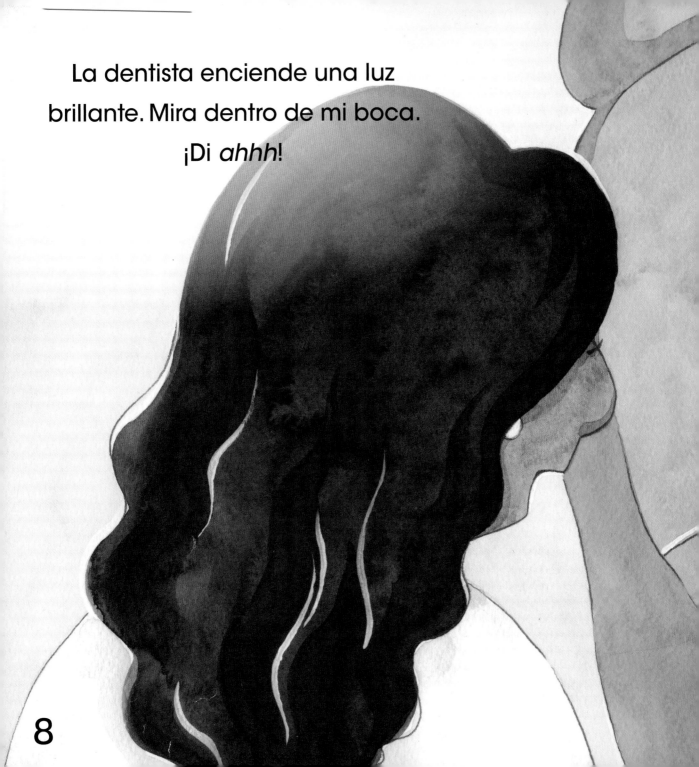

The dentist turns on a bright light. She looks in my mouth. Say ahhh!

9

La dentista dice que mis dientes son de leche.

The dentist says my teeth are called baby teeth.

Algún día me saldrán dientes nuevos.

Some day I will grow new ones.

La dentista dice que mis dientes se ven saludables. ¡Yo cuido mis dientes!

The dentist says my teeth look healthy. I take care of them!

13

La dentista me enseña cómo usar el hilo dental.

The dentist shows me how to floss my teeth.

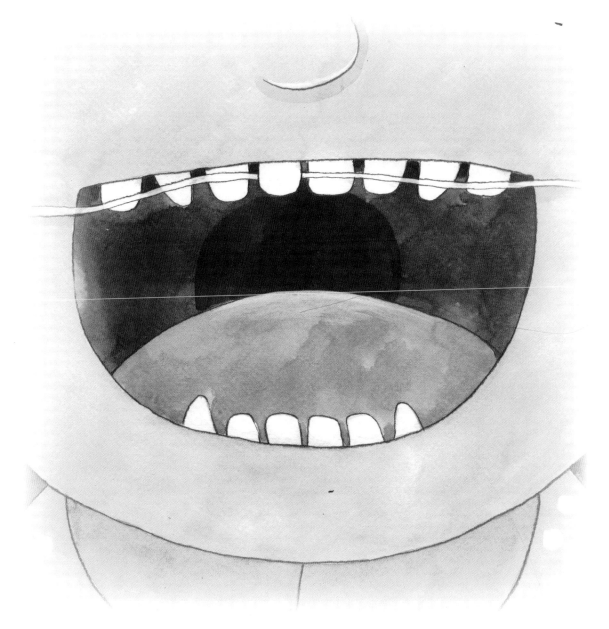

El hilo dental se pasa entre los dientes.

Floss is like a string.

La dentista me muestra cómo cepillarme los dientes.

The dentist shows me how to brush my teeth.

¡Eso yo lo hago bien!

I'm good at this already!

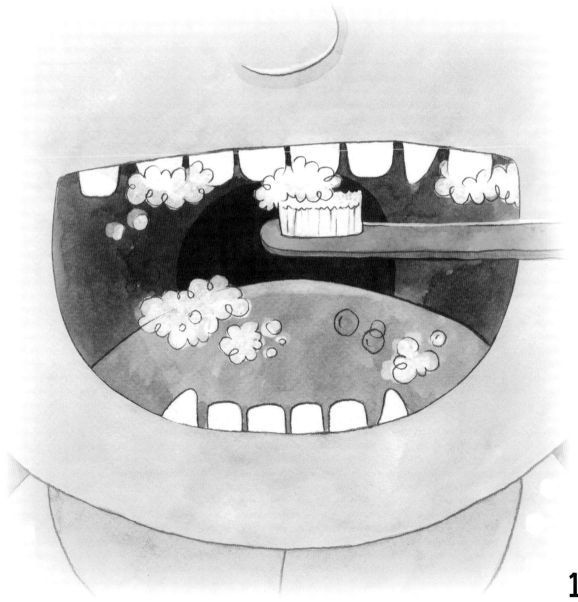

¡Terminamos! Mis dientes están como nuevos dice la dentista.

All done! The dentist tells me
my teeth are like new.

19

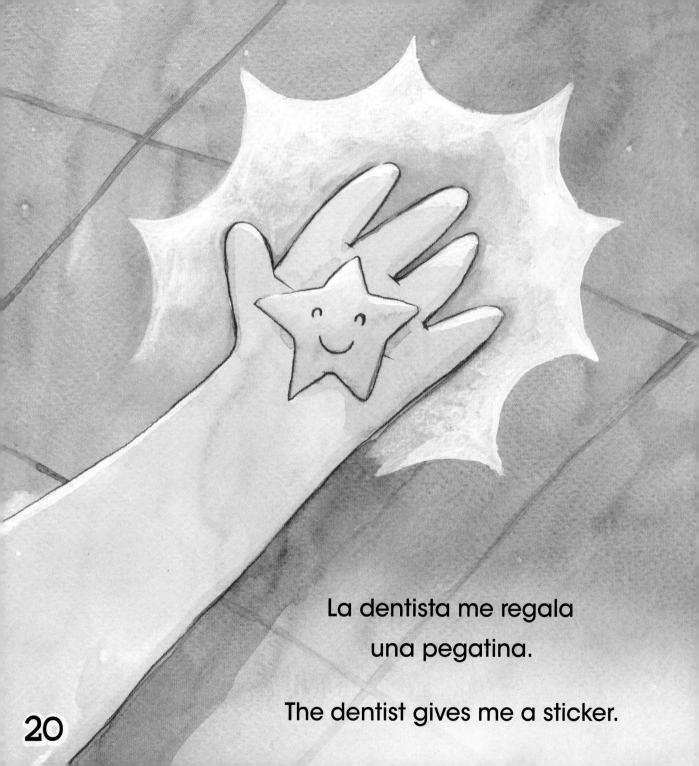

La dentista me regala
una pegatina.

The dentist gives me a sticker.

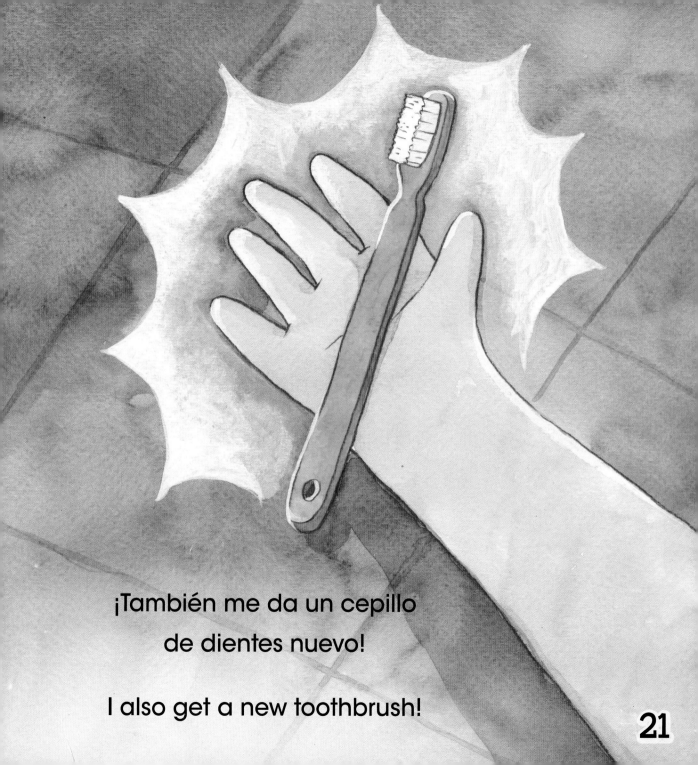

¡También me da un cepillo
de dientes nuevo!

I also get a new toothbrush!

21

Es importante tener
dientes saludables.
¡Me gusta ir al dentista!

It's important to have healthy teeth. I love going to the dentist!

23

Palabras que debes aprender
Words to Know

(el) hilo dental
floss

(los) dientes
teeth

(el) cepillo de
dientes
toothbrush

Índice / Index